Read all of Stanley Lambchop's adventures
by Jeff Brown

Flat Stanley
Stanley and the Magic Lamp
Invisible Stanley
Stanley in Space
Stanley's Christmas Adventure
Stanley, Flat Again!

And lots of new adventures!
by Sara Pennypacker and Josh Greenhut

Flat Stanley: The Japanese Ninja Surprise
Flat Stanley: The Big Mountain Adventure
Flat Stanley: The Great Egyptian Grave Robbery
Flat Stanley: The Epic Canadian Expedition
Flat Stanley: The Amazing Mexican Secret
Flat Stanley: The African Safari Discovery
Flat Stanley: The Flying Chinese Wonders
Flat Stanley: The Australian Boomerang Bonanza
Flat Stanley: The US Capital Commotion

FLAT STANLEY

The US Capital Commotion

Created by **Jeff Brown**
Written by Josh Greenhut
Illustrated by Jon Mitchell

EGMONT

EGMONT

We bring stories to life

The US Capital Commotion
First published in the United States 2011 as
Flat Stanley's Worldwide Adventures #9: The US Capital Commotion
First published in Great Britain 2015
by Egmont UK Limited
The Yellow Building, 1 Nicholas Road
London, W11 4AN

Text copyright 2011 by the Trust u/w/o Richard C. Brown
a/k/a Jeff Brown f/b/o Duncan Brown
Illustrations copyright 2015 by the Trust u/w/o Richard C. Brown
a/k/a Jeff Brown f/b/o Duncan Brown

ISBN 978 1 4052 7250 6

A CIP catalogue record for this title is available from the British Library

Printed and bound in Great Britain by the CPI Group

57771/1

Contents

1   Stars and Stripes   1

2   The Governor's Visit   11

3   A Hero's Welcome   21

4   We the People   31

5   The Monumental Mistake   45

6   The Oval Office   59

7   The Award Ceremony   69

8   In the Mail   81

Stars and Stripes

Every Fourth of July, Stanley Lambchop dreamed of being in the local Independence Day parade – that is, until the year that his bulletin board fell on him in the middle of the night and flattened him.

'Can't I be Abraham Lincoln?' Stanley pleaded. Moments before the parade was about to begin, he found himself sitting in the centre of the Grammar Society float, with his legs rolled up tightly to his chest.

'I cannot tell a lie,' intoned his father, George Lambchop. He towered over Stanley majestically in a white wig and ponytail. 'I think you look patriotic.'

'Oh, George,' blushed Stanley's mother, Harriet Lambchop, who was wearing an old-fashioned blue gown and a ribbon in her hair. 'You are such a good father . . . of our country. George Washington!'

Stanley's father winked. 'No, Betsy Ross. It is you who deserves our gratitude for giving birth to such a fine flag.' He gestured grandly down towards Stanley, and Mrs Lambchop curtsied with a giggle.

'How many times do I have to tell you,' interrupted Stanley, 'I don't want to be the –'

His younger brother, Arthur, appeared from the other side of the float. Arthur had stretched a pale bathing cap over his head and had fringed it with strands from an old grey mop. 'It's not too late to be my kite, Stanley!' He peered down at Stanley from over his tiny spectacles and patted his huge belly, which was actually a pillow stuffed under his shirt.

'I beg your pardon, Mr Benjamin Franklin,' their father said, shaking his head gravely. 'I cannot allow your brother to be struck by lightning.'

'Aw,' said Arthur. 'Even if it means

discovering electricity?'

Suddenly, a nearby brass band launched into a bouncy rendition of 'America the Beautiful'. The float lurched forwards.

'The parade is starting!' Stanley's mother squealed. She picked up a wooden pole and poked it at Stanley. 'Stanley, get up! You have to wave!'

'Can't I just wave with my hands,' Stanley said, 'like everyone else?'

'No!' his family shouted.

Stanley let out a sigh, grabbed on to the top of the pole, and slowly unfurled his body.

His mother had spent days sewing his costume. Thirteen red and white stripes ran down to his toes, while a square of blue with white stars covered half of his chest. He began swishing back and forth, as if he were fluttering in the breeze.

'Check out the Stars and Stripes!' yelled someone.

'Hey, flag boy!' someone yelled. 'Smile!'

A local television crew ran up and hopped alongside the float. Everywhere Stanley looked, people were pointing their fingers at him.

Being flat had given Stanley the opportunity to do things most people never dreamed of. He had travelled around the world by airmail. He could slide under doors, slip between bars, and fold himself into origami ninja throwing stars. He had served as a cape used by the great

matador Carmen del Junco in Mexico and performed with the acrobatic twins known as the Flying Chinese Wonders in Beijing.

But being flat didn't always make Stanley feel good. Sometimes, he felt as if people paid attention to him not because of who he was, but merely because of how he looked. *The only reason everyone is so excited,* thought Stanley, as the float rolled on, *is that I look weird. Nobody cares about what I'm really like.*

Around him, his father, mother, and brother waved excitedly to the screaming throngs of people. Meanwhile, Stanley's body kept on waving, but he didn't even feel like he was there.

★ ★ ★

The next morning, Stanley was examining himself in the mirror that hung on the back of his bedroom door. He turned to the side, and it was as if his body suddenly disappeared. After all, he was only half an inch thick.

Suddenly, the door flew open.

'Guess who's on the front page of the newspaper!' shouted Arthur.

'Thanks for knocking,' Stanley grumbled. He pushed the door, and it swung away from the wall where he'd been abruptly flattened once again.

'It's my room, too,' huffed Arthur. 'Anyway, look!'

Sure enough, there was a photograph of the Lambchops atop the Grammar Society float – and right in the middle was Stanley, swinging from his mother's flagpole. **WHAT A COUNTRY!** blared the headline.

Just then, the telephone rang. 'George,' called Stanley's mother a moment later. 'It's a journalist from WUSA. They're asking about our very own flag – Stanley!'

Stanley felt something rise up from deep inside him. 'I AM NOT A FLAG!' he screamed.

WHAT A COUNTRY!

Arthur gaped at Stanley, and suddenly both their parents were standing in the doorway.

'Stanley,' his mother said slowly. 'Are you feeling all right?'

Without answering, Stanley sprinted straight to the living room and slid under the couch, where nobody could bother him.

The Governor's Visit

The fabric on the couch's bottom bobbed up and down just above Stanley's nose. Arthur was bouncing on it, flipping channels on TV.

'We're on this channel, too!' Arthur cried happily.

Stanley shut his eyes and sighed heavily. *I wish I'd never been flattened,* he thought.

The phone had been ringing all morning. Every time, it was another journalist asking to speak with Stanley, who wouldn't come out from under the couch.

And then the doorbell rang. From his hiding place, Stanley called, 'I'm not here!'

'He's just overwhelmed, George,' he heard his mother murmur.

The doorbell rang again. Stanley heard his father clear his throat, open the door, and say, 'I'm sorry, but –'

Stanley's parents gasped.

'You're not a reporter,' sputtered Mr Lambchop. 'You're – you're –'

'The governor!' a voice boomed. 'And this here is Officer Williams and Officer Parker!'

'Wow,' Arthur's voice whispered. 'Cops.'

'We're here for Mr Stanley Lambchop!' the governor announced.

'You're here for −' Stanley's mother began tentatively.

Stanley's heart raced. *It's the governor! Of the whole state!*

'Well?' boomed the governor. 'Where is he?'

Nobody spoke.

Stanley knew that his family was thinking the same thing he was: Sliding out from beneath a couch is no way to introduce yourself to a very important person.

'I was afraid of this,' murmured the governor. 'Mr and Mrs Lambchop, may we come in?'

Stanley saw a pair of cowboy boots and two pairs of very well-shined shoes stride into view.

'Can you tell us the last time you saw your son, ma'am?' said the black shoes.

'Why, just this morning,' replied Stanley's mother's toe, which was tapping nervously.

'And where was that?' the brown shoes inquired.

'In his room,' answered Mrs Lambchop.

'Great Gettysburg!' murmured the governor's boots. 'They took the boy from his own room! Don't you worry,' the boots declared. 'You can rest assured we will have the full resources of the United States government on the case. Those kidnappers will be sorry they ever thought to mess with an American hero!'

'Kidnappers!?' Mr and Mrs Lambchop cried.

'American hero?' said Stanley.

The cowboy boots and the shined shoes all turned towards the couch.

'Who said that?' whispered the governor.

Stanley poked his head out from under the couch. 'I did?'

'Holy Declaration of Independence!' The governor jumped in surprise.

'I was just, um . . .' Stanley got to his feet. 'Cleaning up underneath the couch.' He picked a piece of fluff off his shirt.

The police officers relaxed their stance, and the governor extended an enormous

hand. 'It's an honour to meet you, young man.'

Stanley shook his hand. 'My mum sewed the costume,' he stammered. 'It really wasn't my idea.'

'Don't be bashful,' said the governor. 'Be proud. We need more heroes like you.'

'But I didn't –'

'America can't get enough of this young man!' He clapped Stanley on the back. 'You're on the cover of every newspaper in the nation!'

'I was Ben Franklin!' interjected Arthur.

The governor mussed Arthur's hair. 'Of course you were! No hero stands alone, my boy!'

Arthur grimaced.

'Stanley, we're here to escort you and your family to Washington. Pack your bags. The chopper lifts off in thirty minutes.'

'Washington, DC?' Mrs Lambchop gasped.

'But why?' said Stanley.

'For the ceremony, of course!' laughed the governor.

The Lambchops exchanged confused looks.

'Wait a second. Are you saying you don't know?'

The governor squared his shoulders officially. 'Stanley Lambchop, by the order of the president of the United States of America, you are to receive the National Medal of Achievement.'

Both of the police officers saluted Stanley.

'Oh, brother,' said Arthur under his breath.

Mr and Mrs Lambchop glared at him. 'Oh, brother,' Arthur repeated, rolling his eyes. *'I'm so proud of you.'*

A Hero's Welcome

The military helicopter zoomed through the sky over America. Inside, the governor briefed the Lambchops.

'The National Medal of Achievement,' the governor explained, 'has been awarded to the greatest scientists, artists, and political leaders in American history, Stanley.'

'But I didn't *do* anything,' Stanley said quietly.

'Leaping Liberty Bell! That's not what I read,' said the governor. 'I read that you saved Mount Rushmore!'

'It was only one of the foreheads,' grumbled Arthur. Stanley nodded in agreement.

The governor punched Stanley's shoulder playfully, and it bent backwards for a moment like the corner of a piece of paper. 'Stanley,' he said admiringly, 'there is nothing more heroic than humility.'

Stanley turned and gazed out of the window. They had passed over yellow prairies and green, rolling hills. Now, they were moments from landing in

Washington, DC. He knew he was supposed to be excited, but he felt that someone had made a terrible mistake.

'You'll be under twenty-four-hour guard during your stay in the capital, Stanley,' said the governor. 'We can't risk an international incident.'

'Do you think Stanley is in danger?' Mrs Lambchop said, shooting an anxious look at Stanley's father.

The governor leaned forwards. 'Did *you* think he was in danger,' he said, 'the night you laid him down to sleep under an innocent-looking bulletin board?'

Stanley's mother's eyes widened.

'Don't worry, we'll take good care of him, ma'am,' said one of the officers sitting behind them.

'Look!' cried Arthur suddenly.

Out the window, the top of a thin white tower loomed, looking close enough to touch.

'The Washington Monument,' said the governor. 'Built to honour our first president, General George Washington. Begun in 1848, and not completed until another forty years later. At the time, it

was the tallest building on Earth. Think of how strange and wonderful it must have seemed. Not a statue of a man on horseback, not a big block of stone carved with words. Just a white pillar tapering to a perfect point, rising over our young country. Such a noble form!'

As the helicopter touched down a few moments later, Stanley glimpsed an enormous crowd of people waving American flags. 'Ready, Stanley?' said the governor.

Stanley had looked into the eyes of sneak thieves while hiding in a painting at the National Museum. He had been kidnapped by spies in Mexico and foiled grave robbers in Egypt.

But he had never been more frightened than this. There was a rustling in his ears, and he realised his whole body was shaking like a leaf.

I shouldn't be here, he thought desperately.

Stanley's parents took his hands as the door swung open, and his feet were immediately blown out from beneath him by the helicopter's rotors. He flapped wildly between his mother and father.

But then the rotors slowed to a stop, and Stanley realised that the roar he was hearing wasn't the helicopter. It was the sea of people before him.

Even more shocking, they weren't waving flags. They were waving ... Stanleys. There were hundreds and hundreds of

posters cut out to look like Stanley in his flag costume.

'Flat Stanley! Flat Stanley! Flat Stanley!' The crowd surged forwards. A screaming girl tried to grab Stanley's head. Someone stepped on his leg, and Stanley imagined a piece of dough being fed into a rolling machine.

I'll be trampled! he thought.

In a panic, Stanley broke free from his parents' grip. He twisted his body and squeezed between two people and then two more, using his flatness to slide through the tight spaces in the crowd. His ears rang with people screaming his name. He slipped and slid and squeezed on and on. Finally, the crowd started to thin out,

and he bent his legs beneath him. Now he was a blur, springing through the air, hopping the way he'd learned from the kangaroos in Australia.

And before he realised what he was doing, Stanley Lambchop was running away.

Chapter Four

We the People

Stanley spotted a pair of police officers strolling towards him. In a panic, he looked around for a place to hide before he was spotted.

Then he saw it: a big framed poster, taller than he was, hung on the side of the building. It showed a crowd of smiling people of every possible shape and shade, wearing traditional garb from all over the world. At the top were the words, WE THE PEOPLE.

The police officers were only a few feet away! Stanley leaped up and balanced inside the frame, plastering his face into a smile. He silently apologised to the white-bearded rabbi he was covering.

WE THE PEOPLE

The police officers were right in front of him when their walkie-talkies crackled.

'Calling all forces! National hero misplaced. Description: eleven years old, less than one inch thick, brown hair. Possible kidnapping.'

'Let's go!' said one of the officers, and they raced away.

Stanley allowed himself to breathe a sigh of relief . . . until he noticed two men on the other side of the boulevard. They were both wearing dark suits and sunglasses, and they were staring right at him. They started crossing the street, weaving between cars, their pace quickening.

Kidnappers! Stanley thought. A chill went down his spine.

At that moment, a crowd of people came marching down the sidewalk, chanting, 'Change the law! Do what's right! Truth and justice must unite!'

Stanley held his breath as he watched the two men start to push their way through the crowd. A placard held high by a marcher, reading AND JUSTICE FOR ALL, slid before his eyes. At the last second

Stanley jumped for it.

Hanging off the back of the sign, Stanley glanced back. The two men were spinning in circles in front of the WE THE PEOPLE poster, shaking their heads, wondering where he had gone.

I need a disguise, Stanley thought.

A block later, Stanley dived into a recycling bin full of newspapers. He started shoving crumpled-up handfuls of

newsprint under his shirt and into the legs of his pants. He'd learned in school how to fold boat-shaped hats out of newspaper, and now he made one and put it on his head.

A tour group was amassed on the giant steps of a building nearby. Stanley rustled up to the back of the group and tried to blend in.

'Many of the most important buildings in Washington were burned during the War of 1812,' the tour guide was saying. 'The Library of Congress was mostly destroyed, as was the Capitol. It is said that the smoke could be seen as far away as Baltimore. Even the White House was ruined – but not before a life-size portrait of George

Washington was cut out of its frame and snuck to safety. And do you know what happened twenty-six hours after the start of the attack, to help scatter the enemy and put out the fires? A tornado struck Washington!'

Stanley gasped. He didn't know that!

'We are very lucky that the most important documents in our nation's history weren't lost during the burning of Washington. Let's go inside the National Archives and see them, shall we?'

Stanley followed the group up the steps.

In a grand room with very high ceilings, Stanley bent over a large piece of yellow parchment, crowded with script. It was the Declaration of Independence, dated the

fourth of July, 1776. The tour guide said it was written by Thomas Jefferson. John Hancock's very fancy signature stood out among the names of all the people who had signed at the bottom. After a moment, Stanley spotted Ben Franklin's signature, among dozens of other spidery names.

The tour guide said that when people first came to America, many of them just wanted to be themselves without getting into trouble. They wanted the right to be different, and that was the first thing that the Declaration of Independence declared: that all people are equal and entitled to life, liberty, and the pursuit of their own happiness.

In the same room, Stanley saw the

Constitution, which set up how the government worked: The president ran things, Congress made laws, and a Supreme Court made tough decisions. The building also had the Bill of Rights, which were the first laws to get passed and are still the most important ones. Right at the beginning, in the First Amendment, there was freedom of speech, freedom of religion, and the freedom to protest.

Stanley was very glad he hadn't been flattened somewhere where it *wasn't* OK to be different. Sure, people sometimes made fun of him; there was a boy at school who had taken to calling him 'Thinbelina'. But he'd never thought he'd get thrown in jail.

'Excuse me,' a small voice said. Stanley turned to see two girls staring at him, holding big, colourful guidebooks. 'My name is Sook-ying and this is my sister, Cho. We are from South Korea. Are you Flat Stanley?'

'No,' Stanley lied.

The girl frowned. 'Your head is flat,' she said. 'Please, we are big fans. May I take a picture with you?'

Stanley smiled. *At least it's OK to be different,* he thought. He put a crinkly, newspaper-filled arm around the girl and smiled.

Just as the camera flashed, Stanley saw two men in black suits and sunglasses appear in the doorway to the giant room.

The kidnappers had tracked him down.

Stanley turned his back and bent his head close to the girls. 'I need your help,' he whispered. His friend Oda Nobu, the famous Japanese movie star, had taught him origami, the art of folding.

A moment later, Stanley spied the men in black as they kicked a mound of scrunched-up newspaper on the floor next to the Bill of Rights. He watched

them as he escaped, sticking out of Sook-ying's backpack, folded up to look like a guidebook.

Chapter Five

The Monumental Mistake

Stanley spent the rest of the day hiding in different museums. He visited the National Gallery of Art, where he hid from the police in three different paintings, including a Picasso. At the Smithsonian National Air and Space Museum, he was admiring the Apollo 11 space capsule, which had landed on the moon, when the

men in black appeared again. Stanley gave them the slip by jumping into an astronaut suit whose visor was open. He found it to be very warm and slightly musty.

In the Smithsonian National Museum of Natural History, Stanley saw the Hope Diamond, an enormous forty-five-and-one-half-carat jewel that was thought to have been cut from the stolen crown jewels of France. *I wish Calamity Jasper could see this,* he thought, thinking of his and Arthur's treasure-hunting friend from Mount Rushmore.

But night eventually fell.

All the museums closed.

And Stanley had nowhere to go.

He saw the Lincoln Memorial shining brightly in the dark, like a lit house on a stormy night. It sat at one end of a large strip of grass called the National Mall.

At the other end, exactly one mile away, was the dome of the US Capitol, where the members of Congress worked. And right in the middle, halfway between the Lincoln Memorial and the Capitol, was the tall white pillar of the Washington Monument.

Stanley settled into Abraham Lincoln's enormous white stone lap and sighed deeply. The statue's big, wise eyes looked unblinkingly over him.

'I've never run away before,' Stanley admitted. 'Everyone must be worried sick.'

Stanley smiled for a moment, thinking of how his mother would correct his grammar. 'Stanley,' she would have said, 'please fix your adverbs. You mean that everyone is sick with worry.'

'But if I go back,' Stanley continued in a soft voice, 'they'll make me out to be some kind of American hero. But I'm *not* one. I'm just a kid who got flattened by a falling bulletin board. Thomas Jefferson wrote the Declaration of Independence even though he knew he was going to get in big trouble with the king of England – that's a hero. Neil Armstrong walked on the moon – that's a hero. Heroes risk everything for what they believe in. They make tough choices, like you did, President Lincoln. I didn't *choose* to be flat. I don't stand for *anything*.'

Stanley looked up at Abraham Lincoln's large, impassive face. And all of the sudden, from a certain angle, the former president looked like the Japanese movie star Oda Nobu, with his big nose and square jaw and beard. Stanley's mind raced back to a moment on a Japanese bullet train, and he could hear Oda Nobu's voice in his mind.

'Stanley-san,' Oda Nobu had said, 'your flatness is what makes you special. But you must remember this: Being flat is *what* you are. It is not *who* you are. *Who* you are is a very bright, very funny, very curious young boy. It is who you are, flat or round. Always remember that, Stanley-san. Flat or round.'

Somehow, the memory made Stanley

feel a little bit better. Maybe he wasn't a hero. But at least he was himself.

Suddenly, a pair of shadows darted across the base of the statue. Stanley stiffened. Before he knew it, he was surrounded by at least a dozen men in black.

'Stanley Lambchop!' one of the men shouted. 'Stop –'

Stanley flipped up into the air and landed on the steps. He sprang end over

end down the grand steps, the men close behind him.

There was a long rectangular pool in front of the Lincoln Memorial. In the darkness, Stanley could see the Washington Monument reflected in and rising above it. Picking up speed, he launched himself over the water and pushed out his stomach.

Stanley skipped on the surface like a

stone: one . . . two . . . three . . . four . . . five times. He started to sink, and began moving his legs like a giant fin, almost as if he were back in Australia, exploring the Great Barrier Reef with Arthur hanging on to his back. Out of the corner of his eye, he could see men in black racing alongside the edge of the pool, their ties flapping over their shoulders.

Stanley at last came to the pool's end. Without stopping, he reared into the air like a snowboard, just clearing two men's heads. He landed and pushed off into a series of kangaroo hops. A man caught his arm, but Stanley slipped from his grasp. The Washington Monument was directly in front of him now.

There were men on either side of it, waiting.

There's no place left to run, thought Stanley. He backed up against the white base of the monument as the men in black slowly closed in.

And then Stanley turned, bent his legs beneath him, and jumped up on to the side of the monument. Because he was damp from the reflecting pool, he stuck to it like a wet washcloth on the side of a bathtub. He took a deep breath and started climbing up.

'Stanley!' one of the men in black called. 'Stop!'

'Why should I listen to a kidnapper like you?!' Stanley shouted back.

Suddenly, Stanley heard a whirring sound, and a suction cup attached to a rope stuck to the monument right next to his head. The rope pulled taut, and one of the men in black started climbing.

Stanley looked towards the sky and continued inching his way up the monument as fast as he could. He would unpeel his arms from the stone, re-stick them a few inches higher up, unpeel the rest of his body, and pull himself up. He felt like an inchworm.

Stanley did not look back. He could hear suction cups with ropes gripping the monument just below him. He kept climbing.

When he finally glanced down, his

stomach lurched. He was more than five hundred feet up. Stanley reached up again, and the stone tilted. He had reached the pyramid-shaped tip of the Washington Monument.

He clung to the surface, panting.

Suddenly, there was a blinding light and a terrible roaring. Stanley trembled as a helicopter rose into view.

'STANLEY LAMBCHOP!' a voice over a loudspeaker boomed. 'STAY WHERE YOU ARE!'

The wind from the helicopter rotor got under Stanley's skin, and his whole body flipped out to the side. He held on to the Washington Monument in desperation, his body flapping like a flag over the capital.

'STANLEY!' the loudspeaker called. 'STOP!'

In his head, Stanley heard the words of Billy Wallaby, the Australian billionaire who had brought him and Arthur to Australia. 'If I were you, I'd worry about the wind, mate. That's the greatest threat to your well-being.'

'Oh no,' Stanley whispered.

His fingers slipped from the stone, and Stanley Lambchop flew through the sky like a shot.

Chapter Six

The Oval Office

A half-mile away, Stanley's back slammed into the dome of the Capitol with a slap. The wind was knocked out of him, and he saw stars. For a moment, he could not even open his eyes.

When he did, there were two men in black crouched over him. Stanley sat up fast, and the side of his head smacked one

of them in the nose.

'Ouch!' the man cried.

The other one held up a badge.

'Secret Service. The president wants to see you,' the man panted.

'You mean you're not kidnappers?' said Stanley.

The men shook their heads.

'You're the good guys?' Stanley said blankly.

The men nodded.

Stanley flopped back down on his back. 'Boy, I'm in big trouble,' he said.

★ ★ ★

The doors opened to the Oval Office. Somebody gave Stanley a light push, and he slinked inside. The doors shut behind him.

At the other end of the room was a big, empty wooden desk, surrounded by windows. A portrait of George Washington looked down at him disapprovingly.

Suddenly, through another door, a woman backed into the room carrying a tray. She turned to face Stanley, and he couldn't believe his eyes.

It was the president herself.

'Hi there, Stanley,' she said, as if they were neighbours. 'You like Mexican food, don't you?'

She put the tray down on a little table in front of a white couch, sat down, scooped some salsa on to a tortilla chip, and popped it into her mouth. She patted the seat beside her.

Stanley didn't move.

'Stanley, the president of the United States just invited you to have a nacho with her.'

Stanley quickly sat down. He carefully took a chip, scooped up some guacamole, and placed it in his mouth.

'Nothing works up the appetite like evading the Secret Service, huh?' the president said.

Stanley swallowed. He looked at his feet awkwardly and shrugged.

'You know, it was I who decided to give you the National Medal of Achievement, Stanley,' said the president. 'It's been awarded to the greatest scientists, artists, and political leaders in American history. It's quite an honour. I thought you really deserved it.'

'Why?'

'Because I think you're someone we can

all look up to,' she said matter-of-factly.

'You mean because I'm flat?' said Stanley.

'No,' replied the president. 'I mean because you use what's different about you to make people all over the world realise what they have in common,' she said. 'You've travelled the globe, showing people that when they have the freedom to be different, they can achieve amazing things.'

Stanley felt himself blushing. 'I haven't done anything amazing,' he said.

The president raised her eyebrows. 'Stanley, I'm the president of the United States of America. I've met a lot of people who have done a lot of important things. But I don't know anyone who has saved Mount Rushmore, foiled an Egyptian antiquities thief, practised martial arts in Japan, gone over Niagara Falls without a barrel, walked across Mexico, unearthed an archaeological fraud in Africa, performed with the Flying Chinese Wonders, flew unaided across Australia – and, as of an hour ago, flapped like a flag hanging off the top of the Washington Monument while the entire world watched, glued to their televisions.'

Stanley smiled. 'That does sound like a lot,' he said.

'Yes, it does,' the president agreed.

Stanley munched some more tortilla chips.

'I do have one question I have been meaning to ask you,' the president said. Her face became very serious. 'I want you to tell me . . . What is La Abuela's secret ingredient?'

Stanley stopped chewing and swallowed hard. With help from the great matador Carmen del Junco, he had travelled across Mexico to discover the famous secret ingredient in La Abuela's cooking. He had sworn he would never reveal it to anyone.

'I'm sorry,' he stammered. 'I can't tell you that.'

'Why not?'

'Because it's a secret.'

The president nodded thoughtfully. 'That's what a hero might say.' She got up, brushed off her pants, and walked towards the door that Stanley had entered from. She turned back to him. 'As long as you always remember that secret, Stanley, and hold it close to your heart, you'll be fine.' She winked.

Stanley thought back to what he had learned in Mexico: The secret is not the ingredient. *It is what you do with it.*

The president looked deep into his eyes, as if to say, *That's why you're here. Because of what you've done with it.*

But how did she know?

'There are some folks who have been very worried about you,' the president said. 'I thought you might like to see them.'

She swung open the doors, and Stanley saw the group of people waiting outside. For a moment, he was speechless. Then he ran up and wrapped his body around each of them, one by one.

The Award Ceremony

The following night, at the famous Kennedy Centre for the Performing Arts, all of those who had travelled to Washington gathered to honour Stanley Lambchop, the youngest and flattest recipient of the National Medal of Achievement in history.

Stanley stood in a special section of seats

above the audience, surrounded by his mother, father, Arthur, and the president herself. He wore a tuxedo crafted by the president's tailor, which made him feel like a special present wrapped in a very thin box. Around his neck, on a red, white and blue-striped ribbon, hung a bronze medallion: the National Medal of Achievement.

When the orchestra finished playing the National Anthem, everyone took their seats. The governor made some brief remarks, and then a girl in a plaid shirt, blue jeans, and a cowboy hat sauntered on to the empty stage. She carried a ukulele.

'My name is Calamity Jasper from the Black Hills of South Dakota,' she said into

the microphone. 'I met Stanley on Mount Rushmore the day he saved Abraham Lincoln's face from cracking off. I'm real proud of him here tonight. This song is for you, cowpoke.'

She gave a few strums of her ukulele and began singing in a sweet, warbling voice. The tune was 'You Are My Sunshine', but she changed the lyrics to 'You are our flat boy, our only flat boy'. She received a standing ovation.

Mr O. Jay Dart, the Lambchops' neighbour and the director of the National Historical Museum, appeared onstage. In great detail, he told the story of how Stanley had caught sneak thieves red-handed in his museum. An enormous screen descended at the back of the stage, and on it was projected a grainy security photograph from that night, clearly showing Stanley dressed as a shepherd girl hiding in a painting. Stanley tried to laugh along with the audience in spite of his embarrassment.

Amisi, the girl who had opened his envelope in Egypt and who had inspired Stanley with her intelligence and sense of justice, recited a beautiful Sufi poem.

Mountie Martin, of the Royal Canadian Mounted Police, showed an instant replay from television of Stanley coiled into a hockey puck, whipping past an NHL goalie to score an impossible goal. When the crowd in the Kennedy Centre jumped

to their feet and cheered, he joked that hockey's most important trophy would now be called the Flat Stanley Cup.

Captain Tony, the African pilot and police officer, stood onstage with his arms around his children, Bisa and Odinga, and told of how Stanley had jumped from his plane with nothing but his body for a parachute.

The billionaire Billy Wallaby stood with

his long-lost brother, Wally Wallaby, and spoke stirringly about Stanley and the spirit of brotherhood.

Oda Nobu, the big Japanese movie star, got up. 'Hello, Stanley-san,' he said. 'You once did me the honour of travelling to Japan, because you said you were a great fan. I am here to return the favour.' A great roll of paper was rolled on to the stage, and Oda Nobu tore off a gigantic sheet that was taller and wider than he was. With great speed and grace, he turned, folded, and flipped the paper this way and that – until suddenly, with a flourish, he held up an origami masterpiece shaped exactly like Stanley in real life!

A tall, dark-haired woman appeared

behind Oda Nobu and held out her slender hand. 'I'll take that,' the great Mexican matador Carmen del Junco said with a sly smile, whisking the intricately folded paper into the air. She swung and swooped the paper Stanley like a matador's cape in grand, dramatic arcs. It was a beautiful performance.

Yin and Yang, the Flying Chinese

Wonders, thanked Stanley for teaching them the secret of balance. They transformed their bodies into a map of the United States, with a fireworks display occurring over it.

As he clapped, Stanley turned excitedly to his brother – but he wasn't there. 'Where's Arthur?' he whispered to his mother. At that moment, he was surprised to see Arthur shuffling across the stage to the microphone.

'My name's Arthur Lambchop,' Arthur said, as the applause died down. 'I'm Stanley's little brother.'

The microphone was way too tall for him, and he had to stand on his tiptoes to make himself heard. 'It's not always easy having a brother like Stanley. People pay more attention to him. That's just the way it is. Plus, he gets to do stuff that my mum and dad wouldn't let me do in a million years.'

You could hear a pin drop in the theatre, and Stanley saw his parents exchange worried looks.

'But,' Arthur continued slowly, 'I remember when we went with my dad to Africa, and Stanley got really upset

because he felt alone. He was sad because there were no flat people like him. And all I could think was that nobody makes me feel less alone than my brother. He's like . . . he's like the glue that you didn't even know was there between people, the thin layer bonding all of us together. When you're a kid and people ask you who your hero is, they mean, "Who do you want to be like when you grow up?" And I . . . I hope I can be as honest, flexible, and strong as my brother.'

Stanley felt a lump in his flat throat like a golf ball.

'I love you, Stanley. You're my hero.'

Chapter Eight

In the Mail

At a party in a grand ballroom after the ceremony, Arthur paced before the line of people like a general. Stanley was on the end.

'OK, people! Quiet!' Arthur said. 'This is it! Ready?'

A murmur of excitement went down the line. Yang, the Flying Chinese Wonder, leaned forwards and winked at Stanley. Stanley noticed that, beside him, Carmen del Junco and Oda Nobu were holding hands.

'Commence countdown!' hollered Arthur. 'Ten, nine, eight, seven, six, five, four, three, two . . . one!'

Yin flipped high into the air and landed on her brother Yang's shoulders. Yang bent his knees, and the pair launched straight upwards like a rocket. Yang landed on Oda Nobu's shoulders, so they were now three people tall. At that moment, Carmen del Junco grabbed Stanley's hands and spun him around. His feet left the ground, and she let go. Stanley arced around the room like a boomerang, until he saw Yang's face come into view, and they grabbed each other's hands.

Stanley held his body out to the side and waved his legs gently atop the flagpole formed by his friends.

The rest of the people down below whooped and hollered.

'That's my boy!' cried his father.

'Bravo!' yelled the president of the United States.

'Be careful!' cried Stanley's mother.

High over his friends from all over the world, Stanley waved his body proudly.

'Now me!' called Arthur.

Two months later, Arthur and Stanley were playing in their room at home when their mother burst in. 'Look!' she cried, waving an enormous envelope.

'What is it?' asked Stanley.

'Open it!' said his mother.

The envelope was made of thick, creamy paper, and Stanley slipped his finger under the flap and slit it open.

He pulled out a grand square of paper and read:

You are cordially invited
to join us in celebrating our
wedding
Oda Nobu
of Tokyo, Japan
y
Carmen del Junco
of Mexico City, Mexico

In the corner of the invitation was a note jotted in blue pen. Stanley peeked inside the envelope and spotted something else inside. He pulled out a piece of card that was shaped just like a very small version of himself.

'What's that?' said Arthur.

'RSVP via Flat Stanley,' Stanley read.

'You're starting a trend,' Arthur said. He sounded impressed.

Stanley smiled to himself and walked over to his bulletin board. He looked for a free spot among all of the things tacked up there. His eyes passed over a newspaper headline from when he saved Mount Rushmore, pinned next to a postcard from Calamity Jane. There was a snapshot of him and Amisi in front of Egyptian pyramids and a picture of Oda Nobu in a karate class in Japan. Partially hidden behind one corner of an Australian boomerang, there was a picture from the Beijing Zoo of Stanley with a ferocious-looking panda bear. There was a newspaper headline from his plunge over Niagara Falls next to a flat fish head skull from Africa. He'd had a lot of adventures, and he hoped to have many more. In the centre of the board, with its red, white, and blue ribbon hanging from a pushpin, was his National Medal of Achievement.

Stanley grabbed a free pushpin and tacked the wedding invitation next to the bronze medal. He read again the note jotted in the corner:

Stanley,
Thank you for bringing us together.

Amazing things can happen when you're flat! Stanley Lambchop was just a normal healthy boy, but since a large notice board fell on him, he's been only half an inch thick.

Stanley gets rolled up, sent in the post, flown like a kite and helps catch two dangerous art thieves. He may be flat, but he's a hero!

Flat Stanley by Jeff Brown

The original classic adventure

A FLAT STANLEY ADVENTURE

Read all of Flat Stanley's adventures!